What's Your Something Special?

Author, Catherine Gibson
Illustrator, Mary Fletcher

For Children With Love Publications

Illustrations by Mary Fletcher

Gibson, Catherine (Catherine Czerwinski)
   What's Your Something Special? / author, Catherine Gibson ; illustrator, Mary Fletcher.

   pages : color illustrations ; cm

   Summary: Samantha longs to be just like everyone else, but she is special. She wonders if she is only special for what she can't do--walk. Is this all that makes her unique? If so, she doesn't want to be special anymore. Beth is the only friend that understands because Beth is different too. One summer night, a mysterious magician offers a gift to Samantha that will change forever how she sees herself and her friend.
   "A portion of the proceeds from each book sold is donated to the For Children With Love Foundation which supports children's causes."
   Interest age level: 006-008.
   ISBN: 978-0-9831221-2-8

   1. Individual differences in children--Juvenile fiction. 2. Children with disabilities--Psychology--Juvenile fiction. 3. Self-perception in children--Juvenile fiction. 4. Magicians--Juvenile fiction. 5. Individuality--Fiction. 6. People with disabilities--Psychology--Fiction. 7. Self-perception--Fiction. 8. Magicians--Fiction. I. Fletcher, Mary, 1954- II. Title.

PZ7.G339264 Wh 2014
[Fic]

ISBN 978-0-983-12212-8

TXu-1-890-429

For Children With Love
P.O. Box 1552
Farmington, Connecticut 06034

www.forchildrenwithlove.com

Printed in the USA

What's Your Something Special?

Author, Catherine Gibson

Illustrator, Mary Fletcher

For Children With Love Publications
Farmington, Connecticut

A portion of the proceeds from each book sold is donated to the
For Children With Love Foundation which supports children's causes.
visit www.forchildrenwithlove.com

"You can't catch me!" I heard someone shout. It was the last day of school and, as usual, I was looking out at the other kids playing at recess.

I'd often wondered how it would feel to follow my friends in a chase. What would it be like to climb the ladder or to swing from the monkey bars? I would grab onto one bar as I let go of another, while my feet walked through the air.

But, I'm not able to run or climb or even walk one step. I'm in a wheelchair. I can't do these things because my legs don't move.

The bell rang at the end of the day. All the excited children rushed past me down the crowded hallway. They knew that summer vacation would start as soon as they ran through the school doors.

While I waited outside for my ride, my friend, Beth, tapped me on the shoulder.

"What's wrong, Samantha?" she asked.

"Nothing," I said at first. But Beth kept looking at me.

"I wish I could play with other kids on the playground," I finally admitted.

Beth nodded, "So do I. No one plays with me, either. I guess they think it's strange that I sit alone drawing all the time, even at recess..."

I looked up at her. Maybe I wasn't the only one who felt so alone.

"Hey, Sam," she said, "Do you think we could spend some time together this summer?"

"Sure!" I said quickly.

"Great! Gotta go," Beth shouted as she ran for her bus.

When my mom came, she lifted me into the back seat of the van.

"So how's my special kid?" Mom asked.

"I don't want to be a special kid anymore," I grumbled. "That just means I'm different. I'm special for what I can't do—I can't walk! Everyone else is special for what they can do. I just want to be the same... the same as everyone else."

Mom wrapped her arms around me and held me close.

"Oh Samantha," she whispered, "Just like everyone else, you are unique."When you find the something special that you hold inside, you'll also have the key to share it with others."

On the way home, Mom glanced at me now and then in the rearview mirror.

Finally she said, "Samantha, you may never walk, but there are so many things you can do. You have a wonderful imagination. That's why you can write such beautiful poems and stories." That's something very special about you. Your family, friends and teachers can help guide you, but only you have the key within your heart to make it happen.

"Okay, Mom," I murmured, staring out the window. But I had heard it all before.

When we turned the corner, I saw a huge billboard that made my spirits soar!

"Mom ... Mom, look at that! A circus is in town. I've never been to a circus before. Please, can I go with Beth?" I asked excitedly.

"Well", Mom answered slowly, "I'm not so sure if ... well, okay. I would be happy to take you and Beth to the circus."

That night I called Beth. She was so excited. It was all we could talk about for days and days!

Finally, it was the big night. We sat under the circus tent, eating pink cotton candy and nibbling fresh popcorn, waiting eagerly for the show to begin. The lights dimmed and the music came up.

The ringmaster thundered:

"Ladies and gentlemen, the most amazing show of the century is about to begin…"

So many things began to happen at once!

Clowns with huge feet frolicked and tumbled. A glittering performer stood gracefully on a horse galloping around the ring.

There were trapeze artists flying over my head.

Then the ringmaster announced:

"…and now for the most magnificent magician ever to dazzle your eyes…"

A mysterious man swirled his silk cape and a fierce looking tiger leaped out of a cloud of smoke. A second later, the tiger vanished only to reappear in the center ring. We watched wide-eyed as one spectacular act after another took place.

When the show was over, the crowd poured out into the cool night air. I was surprised to see the magician performing outside. A small group had gathered around him, but he looked past them when he saw Beth wheeling me toward him.

He bent down and asked, "How did you enjoy the show?"

Beth giggled with her hands over her mouth.

I said softly, "I— I believe in you. I believe in your magic. Can I be in the circus one day? Can I fly on the trapeze?"

The magician smiled sadly. "Wait here for me," he said, swirling his cape. He lit up with bright sparks of color. Then he disappeared into a puff of gray smoke.

It was not long before the magician appeared once again out of the same cloud of smoke. He pulled an object from his cape and gave it to me.

"Sunglasses?" I asked, a little disappointed. "Are they magic?"

"No," he admitted. "But they can help you to see what you have never seen before."

"I don't need any help seeing!" I grumbled.

"At times, we all need help seeing," the magician said mysteriously.

He slipped the glasses over my eyes and began to recite these words:

When you find your something special
You'll know it right away
It comes from deep inside you
And never goes away.

It's something you've always had
But can't find in a book
Don't give up, just try again
Take another look.

There is a special gift
That only you can share
The more you give from your heart
The more you'll find is there.

When you look inside yourself
Believe in what you see
You'll find your special something
Your heart will hold the key.

Then he swirled his cape around him and was gone.

On the way back home, Beth chattered excitedly about the magician. I sat quietly, hearing the magician's words playing in my head like a song. Did I have something special? If so, what was locked inside of me? And where was the key?

When we pulled into Beth's driveway, we hugged and said good-bye.

As we drove away, I slipped on the sunglasses and closed my eyes. I put my hand out the open window and felt the cool air blow through my fingers. I felt like a bird circling high above. Then I became a trapeze artist flying through the air!

My wheelchair was nowhere in sight.

That night as I sat in my wheelchair, in my bedroom, I kept the sunglasses on even though I could hardly see at all in my dark room. I took them off and wondered if there was a button to push or a switch to make them work.

With a sigh, I tried them on again, tightly closing my eyes.

"Oh, I wish I could find the key inside of me." I said out loud. "I wish I could run ... and climb ... and fly on a trapeze!"

But, my legs still didn't move.

I ripped the sunglasses off and flung them across the room.

I covered my face with my hands and cried, "Where ... where is the key inside of me?"

I wiped my tears and saw that the sunglasses had landed near my bed. I wheeled my chair over to get them, but they were just out of my reach. I leaned closer, scooting to the edge of my wheelchair.

Leaning as far as I could, I inched my fingers across the floor. I came closer and closer ... until I felt the smooth edge of the rim. But each time I tried to grab the sunglasses, I pushed them farther away.

"Oh, no," I cried, "I can't do it. I can't do anything!"

Out of nowhere, the magician's words came to me, "Don't give up..."

I tried one last time, reaching even farther than before. At last they were in my grasp!

I did it! The sunglasses were in my hand!

I sat back, clutching my sunglasses with a sigh of relief.

At that moment, the phone rang.

It was Beth. Her voice sounded soft and sad.

"What's wrong?" I asked.

With a sniffle, she said, "I loved going to the circus so much, I wanted to draw it for you, Sam. But my drawing was not coming out how I wanted it to! Then I pressed too hard and tore a big hole in the paper!"

"Oh, Beth," I said, "I understand how you're feeling. For different reasons we feel the same way!"

I told her how I threw my sunglasses across the room. It wasn't long before we were giggling. I let her know that I thought she was the best artist in the school because she draws straight from her heart.

"When I write my stories, Beth, will you draw the pictures for me?" I asked.

"Really, Sam?" she asked softly.

"Sure," I said. "You've got something special!"

When I got off the phone, Mom was standing at my door. She must have heard me talking with Beth.

"Mom," I said, "these sunglasses aren't really magic at all. But they did help me to see that there's magic in believing in myself. I love to write! If I believe with all my heart, I can do so much more than I ever thought was possible. That is the key! I found it when I helped Beth see what was special about her."

Mom nodded and smiled.

"Samantha," she said, "long ago when you were in the car accident, we thought we might lose you. But, you made it through because you are strong. Your gifts are more than physical. You can use your words to help others realize that they can do wonderful things. With your writing, you can inspire others to look inside their hearts to find their special gifts."

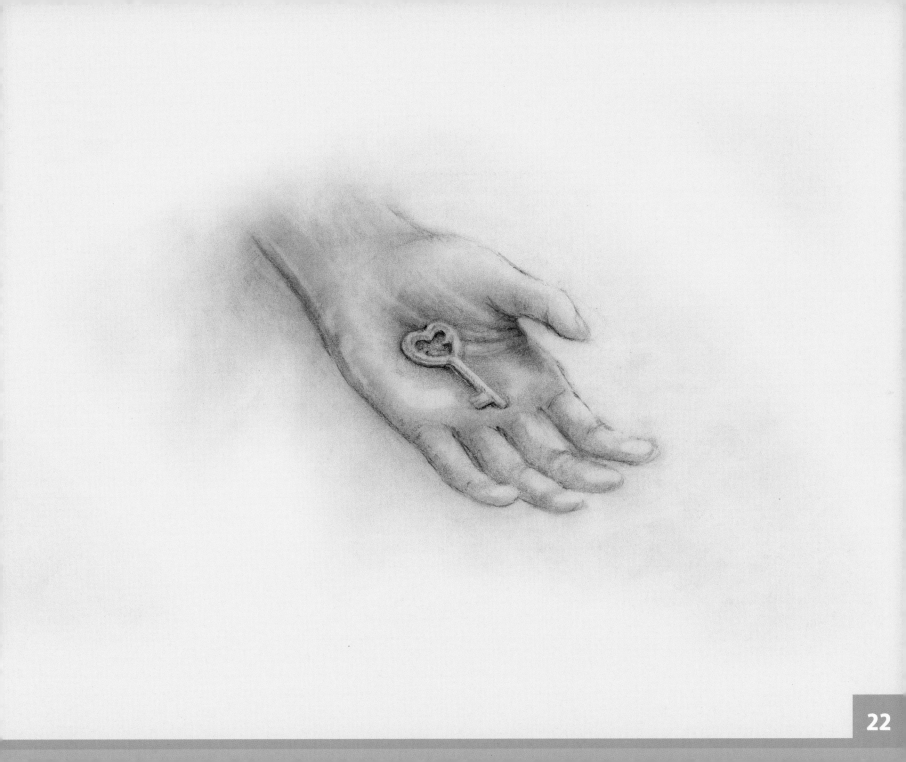

Early the next morning, I sat at my desk in the bedroom, holding the sunglasses in my hand. Through the sunlit window, I saw my reflection.

I put down the sunglasses and started to write: Everyone has a gift inside. When you believe in yourself, anything is possible. The key is within your heart...

I laughed a little at myself and kept smiling as I hummed the magician's rhyme like a song over and over.

When you find your something special
You'll know it right away
It comes from deep inside you
And never goes away.

It's something you've always had
But can't find in a book
Don't give up, just try again
Take another look.

There is a special gift
That only you can share
The more you give from your heart
The more you'll find is there.

When you look inside yourself
Believe in what you see
You'll find your special something
Your heart will hold the key.

What's Your Something Special?

_____

_____

_____

_____

_____

_____

_____

_____

_____

_____

_____

_____

To my sons Tyler & Stefan

*Follow
your
dreams
xoxo mama*

Thank You

To Scott Sierakowski for the computer magic he performs
turning the pictures and words of my stories into pages.

Photographer Michael D Miller Photography